The Gentleman's Guide to Getting Lucky

The Gentleman's Guide to Getting Lucky

KATHERINE TEGEN BOOKS

An Imprint of HarperCollins Publishers

Katherine Tegen Books is an imprint of HarperCollins Publishers.

The Gentleman's Guide to Getting Lucky
Copyright © 2019 by Mackenzie Van Engelenhoven

ISBN 978-0-06-296717-6

Typography by Carla Weise
Map by David Curtis
20 21 22 23 24   PC/LSCH   10 9 8 7 6 5 4 3 2 1
❖
First trade paperback edition, 2021

To all the fan fiction that gave me the sex education
I never got in school

Our love has passed through the shadow and the night of estrangement and sorrow and come out rose-crowned as of old. Let us always be infinitely dear to each other, as indeed we have been always.

—Oscar Wilde to Alfred Bosie Douglas

The Gentleman's Guide to Getting Lucky

ONE

"Do you mean to tell me that you have not actually fornicated yet?"

"Dear God, Felicity." I lunge across the beach in an attempt to clap a hand over her mouth, and miss entirely. She is farther down the beach than I thought. The heavy copy of *Don Quixote* she dug up from a bookstore in Oia that's sitting on my chest tumbles to the ground with a dull *flump*. Felicity, unimpressed by my pounce, retrieves my book, shakes the sand out from between its pages, then returns it to me with a disapproving scowl, as if I am the one behaving inappropriately by dropping a book, when it's she who is shouting about my sex life.

"Oh please. They're too far out to hear." Her eyes flit

across the bay, where two dark heads are poking up from the surf—Ebrahim and Percy, treading water while they wait for Georgie to finish his scramble up the side of the cliff, then leap off and join them in the ocean. She leans back against a piece of driftwood, letting her copy of *Paradise Lost* fall closed on one finger. "You're certainly taking your time."

"It's only been a month."

"*Only?*" She arches an eyebrow. My regret that I even toed this subject with her intensifies. "I expected that once you and Percy were in agreement about living in sin, you would lean hard into it."

Over the waves, I hear a loud whoop of delight, and Felicity and I both look up as Georgie leaps with his knees pulled up to his chest. The water throws the sun's reflection into my eyes before I can see his splash, and I hold *Don Quixote* up as a shield. In spite of our month in Santorini, as a lad raised beneath the dishwater-gray skies of England, I was not prepared for just how hot the weather can be, nor how quickly the bastard sun burns me. I'm also still adjusting to sand perpetually in my shoes and the hems of my trousers, and the murderous havoc these rough, hilly streets have wreaked on my calves—there's not yet been a day I haven't risen from my bed stiff as an old man. Though I could live happily forever on this diet of Cyclades beaches and domed roofs bluer than the sky and grapefruits picked from our courtyard for breakfast, halved and salted and spraying sticky juice that stays on my fingers all day. With the scheduled departure of the *Eleftheria* delayed, first by a buyer for their cargo in Crete, then by a repair to the mizzenmast after a storm on the return journey cracked it, Felicity, Percy, and I have been treated to far more of a holiday here than originally anticipated.

Though a single addition to this Paradise could vastly improve it.

"Well, I was certainly ready to shake sheets straightaway," I say, falling backward onto the beach again and letting the book rest open over my eyes. "But Percy's a bit of a proper young lady, turns out."

"What do you mean by that?" Felicity asks. "If that's meant to be an insult, it's in poor taste."

I laugh. "To whom? You're hardly a proper young lady."

"There are many ways to be proper, you know. And don't do that." She snatches the book off my eyes, and

I recoil with a caw of surprise. "You'll break the spine. You're supposed to be reading it, not using it as a visor."

"It keeps the sun from my eyes."

"If the sun is in your eyes, move into the shade."

I squint at her. "But I like the sun."

"Fine." She sets *Don Quixote* carefully upon the log behind her, then brushes her hands off on her skirt. "See if Percy loves you when you're red as a cherry."

"Percy would love me if I were green and purple." I have to resist the urge to reach up and scratch the space where my right ear used to be. The burns there have begun to heal into scars, so I've started experimenting with a variety of increasingly creative ways to hide this uninvited alteration to my face. Though short of adopting some sort of masked vigilante persona, it's beginning to feel futile to do anything other than simply learn to live with the way I now look. It has been a not insignificant adjustment. I'm still shy around mirrors— even very polished cutlery can be disarming. Still catch myself wondering why noise in a crowd is so hard to pick apart. Still go to push my hair behind my ear and get an unpleasant lurch over finding it absent, nothing left but raised marks in furious red.

Dear God, in spite of the grapefruits, this deaf, sex-less month has been an eternity.

"So what's Percy done that's got your breeches twisted?" Felicity asks, *Paradise Lost* once again open as though to prove just how little she cares about this conversation, but it's her dragging it out again, not me.

"Nothing—that's the problem." I flip over onto my stomach, elbows buried in the sand. "He's never *done* anything. With anyone. And he's more tentative about it now than he was when he was tipsy in Venice. Should have seized that opportunity."

A soft wind snakes off the water, and Felicity claps a hand to the back of her floppy hat to keep it from blow-ing away. "Now, *that* makes you sound like a pig."

"He wasn't *very* tipsy—just enough to feel brave about getting a hand down my breeches and taking me by the—"

"Stop." She bats a handful of sand at me. "I don't need details."

"And I'm fairly certain he's ready now, but I don't know how to bring it up anymore. How do you mention sex like it doesn't matter?"

"Does it?" she asks. "Given your history, I would

have thought you'd be quite cavalier about it."

"It matters to Percy. And because of my *history*, as you so generously termed it, I don't want him to think I'm rushing him into it. *And* there's never a good moment! We've got that flat stuffed full of pirates, and you're always lurking—"

"I resent that choice of words."

"And it's not the most romantic place—I stepped on a cockroach this morning when I got out of bed; did I tell you that?"

"I know, I heard you scream. The pitch was remarkable."

"And this whole island is only about eight feet square." I roll over again, my head falling backward in the most champagne-colored despair. "I hate this."

Felicity licks her finger to turn a page. "Hate what? Chastity?"

"Emphatically yes. I have a reputation."

"For getting trousers off in a timely fashion? Not sure that's one worth defending in order to prove your fidelity to Percy."

"I mean I've got a reputation for running around a

lot, and Percy thinks I know what I'm doing."

"Well, you do. Don't you?" She actually looks up at me for the first time, overtop of her spectacles. "Dear Lord, you haven't been a virgin all this while, have you?"

"No, but I'm a bit concerned my virginity is starting to grow back."

"That is not how any of this works."

"Perhaps I'm a miracle of science. And if we are to be casting off as soon as Scipio expects, we need to do it before we leave, or I will well and truly begin to gnaw my own fingers off over the course of two months at sea with no privacy. And also I just really, really want to blow him."

"All right, that's enough reasons, thank you."

She goes back to staring at her book, but I can tell she isn't reading. Her gaze is fixed upon a spot at the top of the page, teeth working her bottom lip. I close my eyes, partly because the goddamn sun is pointing straight into them and partly because I'm overdue for a nap, but then Felicity asks, "What if I helped you?"

I open one eye. "With what?"

"With your lack of sexual relations," she replies frankly.

I'm not sure if I want to laugh or throw up on her. "No. Don't take that the wrong way, but . . . absolutely, definitely no. Let me say it once more, just to be certain you heard: No. I don't need you getting Percy warmed up for me."

The wind folds the brim of her hat over her face again, but I can feel the vibration of her eye roll. "Not like that, you pervert. What if I clear out the flat so you and Percy can have some time alone? I'll make certain you aren't disturbed, so you won't have to worry about being discreet, and we can create some sort of ambiance to offset the roaches."

I hadn't thought of any of this. Whenever and however our inaugural unholy union occurred, I knew it mattered to Percy because it was not only our first, but his first. But I certainly hadn't considered making a spectacle of the evening. Sex had always been something quick and informal and usually done standing up in the deserted hallway off a barroom or behind my mother's hibiscus bushes. Not something that required any kind of production value. "What do you mean by that?" I ask.

She shrugs. "You know, dress up the flat a little. Get some good wine and nice-smelling perfume and spread rose petals about."

"Roses make Percy sneeze."

"Well then, we shall substitute very finely chopped potatoes."

"You're such a romantic."

Her chin rises. "Do you want my help or not?"

"The idea of you helping me with this in any way is upsetting."

"Fine." She turns the page, though it's almost certainly just for the drama of it. "Remain virtuous and frustrated."

Silence for a moment. Then, before I can stop myself, I ask, "Do I need to do all of that? Roses and wine and . . . do I have to touch the roaches to get them out?"

Felicity doesn't look up from her book. "You don't *have* to."

I can hear the unspoken conclusion—*but you should.* I blow a piece of hair out of my eyes and stare up at the cloudless sky. This is getting more complicated than I anticipated.

And it already felt really goddamn complicated.

There's a splash, and Felicity and I both raise our heads as Percy stumbles up the beach, dripping wet and shaking water from his hair like a dog. He's wearing nothing but his breeches, which the ocean has slung low on his hips and pasted to his legs, rendering him a veritable anatomical study. He's got this little bit of softness at the base of his stomach that stops my heart, and his dark skin is speckled with sand, making a starry sky of his bare chest to match the freckles beneath his eyes.

He's breathless from the swim and swipes his hair out of his eyes as he flops down on his stomach beside me, spraying seawater. Felicity, though certainly too far away to feel the splash, shelters her book. "Come have a swim with me," Percy says, pressing his face into my arm and biting affectionately.

"No thank you," I say, for not only do I loathe putting my head beneath the water, but also there are several reasons why I had best not remove my trousers at this moment. Though I'm not sure they're doing much good to hide the fact that I am very much enjoying the sight of him slick and salty from the sea.

"Come on." He snuffles his face into my shoulder, which I think he's trying to disguise as affection when really he's using me as a towel. "I'll teach you how to float."

"Montagues aren't made to float," I reply. "We're far too sturdy."

"Built like corgi dogs," Felicity adds, her eyes fixed determinedly on her book.

"Corgi dogs float." Percy rolls onto his back, pulling my arm under him. He's drowsy and silly with the afternoon spent in the sun-warmed water, his skin sticking to mine everywhere we touch. "Come jump with me."

I let out a bark of laughter. "You think I will jump off *that* cliff"—I tip my head at the offending land mass—"into *that* ocean?"

"Come on. Just once."

"I'm . . ." I look around for an excuse other than *cowardly*. "Reading." I snatch up *Don Quixote* so fast I almost knock Felicity's hat off, and throw it open for emphasis, realizing too late that it's upside down.

"That seems false. Felicity?" Percy tosses a lump of damp sand at her. "Come have a swim?"

"I am *actually* reading," she replies.

Percy lets out a dramatic sigh, then climbs to his feet. He makes one last attempt to pull me up after him, but I do not concede. The only thing stronger than my love for Percy is my hatred of the goddamn ocean, which is dark and deep and much, much stronger than I am. He gives up, flicks his wet fingers in my face so I flinch with a laugh, then saunters away, back to the water. He makes the walk with such deliberate slowness that I'm almost sure he knows just how fantastic his ass looks in those wet breeches and is trying to use it as a siren song to lure me in after him.

Be strong! I command myself. Odysseus resisted the Sirens! Did he? I don't remember. I slept through most of my literature lessons at Eton. But I am almost positive none of his Sirens had an ass that fantastic.

As soon as Percy is in the water again, I toss *Don Quixote* onto the sand and scoot closer to Felicity. "All right, fine, yes. Help me."

She doesn't even glance up. "Don't sound so grateful for it."

"Your involvement in my intimate activities requires no gratitude on my part." From beyond the waves, I can hear Percy laugh as he swims out to Ebrahim and Georgie. The sound makes me feel like sunshine.

Very sexually frustrated and half-hard sunshine.

"But I am desperate. And you are the only one available."

She snorts. "Bet you say that to all the girls."

TWO

Aside from the chastity, Percy's and my first stretch of togetherness has been a delirious, gauzy dream. A stupidly picturesque setting with this gorgeous gent, and goddamn I would have had him the first time we kissed in earnest, up to our waists in the Aegean Sea, but for the fact that I had recently lost half my hearing and the whole of my ear, and I was not in a state that was conducive to any sort of strenuous and prolonged physical activity. And when it does happen, I intend it to be strenuous and prolonged and deeply physical. So instead of shattering the commandments on the spot, we had lounged upon the beach that day and talked, at great length and—at last—with great honesty and also a good number of recesses when one of us would lean over and offer the other something better to do with his mouth.

It had felt like the first deep breath I'd ever taken, to tell him everything, to hear his half of it all, then hold them up together to find they fit like two pieces of cracked pottery. I wanted so badly to go back in time and give us both a good scolding for not using our words earlier and explaining to each other we were both hungry for the same thing. We could have been going on years coupled rather than years of lonely torment.

But that's part of our story, I suppose. It seems shinier and more spectacular here and now, and after everything.

That night, I had lain in bed atop the blankets, twitchy and wakeful in a room so humid that beads of condensation were forming upon the plaster walls. I stared at the ceiling for what felt like hours, sweating off years of my life and wondering if I had imagined the whole brilliant day, beached on the Aegean. I kept touching my fingers to my lips, feeling the raw, tender skin there to remind myself that yes, it had, yes, he had, yes, we had.

But perhaps the next time I saw Percy, away from the glorious shine of the sunlight on the water, we'd be bashful and private again, or he would decide that confessions of love and fidelity and a life together were foolish. I had kissed my fair share of lads who had only used me as a counterpoint to their own virtue. My primary contribution to our circles back home had been making everyone else feel grounded and well-behaved in comparison.

Or maybe I couldn't live up to my grand words. Maybe I could never be the version of myself I wanted for Percy, no matter how hard I tried or how much of a reformed rake I aspired to be. That hateful, selfish streak I was struggling to tamp may be as much a part of me as my own heart. I wasn't sure what I'd do when he realized that. Somehow, letting our feelings out into the light had both eased so many of my fears and created an entirely new set that kept sleep at bay.

The flat had settled for the night. The chatter from a dice game downstairs had quieted, and only the cicadas and the swoosh of the ocean underscored the silence. I thought of getting up for a drink to calm me enough to sleep, but even excusing it as medicinal did not seem the best way to start off my new resolution to experience all my feelings sober. Which, as it happens, is really goddamn hard. I was still battling the want when the floorboards outside my room creaked. Then I heard the door open, followed by a silence so long I thought I had imagined it, another strange new auditory hallucination resulting from losing my hearing.

I sat up, and there was Percy in the doorway. When I moved, he jumped and clapped a hand to his chest.

"Were you pretending to sleep?" he hissed.

"No, I didn't realize you were lurking."

"I'm not lurking. I'm . . . thinking."

"Well, do you want to come do your thinking in here?" I scooted toward the wall and patted the empty space in the bed beside me.

He stood still for a moment, then shut the door behind his back before making his way to the bed, tentative and shy like he was crossing a ballroom to ask me to dance. When he lay down, we were face-to-face, so close we were sharing our breath, until I rolled over so I could hear him clearly if he spoke. There was a pause, then he slid an arm around my waist and pulled me to him; his body fit against mine like we were a set of quotation marks. With both of us in our nightshirts, I could feel his bare knees against the backs of mine, his legs so long that he had to press his toes against the bottoms of my feet or else they'd hang off the end of the bed. My fingers slid between his as they found their rest around my waist. And God, I was so happy just to be with him, but also, God, I really wished we were doing this oiled up and with no clothes on, and I could not understand how those two things could exist so equally weighted inside me.

I felt his breath against the back of my neck when he leaned in, nose brushing the top of my spine, and I was sure he would whisper something soft and romantic, or, even better, perhaps an invitation to have him right then and there.

But instead he whispered, "Monty . . . are you flexing?"

"What?" Thank God it was dark, for I felt myself go red to my toes. "Of course not."

"Christ, you are *shameless*."

"Well, I'm trying to impress you!"

"Oh, is *that* it?" He pressed a knuckle into my ribs, right in the spot he knows tickles, and I squirmed with a laugh, my stomach going soft. He tried to smother my cackle with a hand clapped over my mouth, but I leaned into a childhood habit before I could resist and I bit him. He let go with a yelp.

"Unhand me, you rogue."

"You're an animal." He kissed me on the back of the neck, then pressed his forehead to the same spot. "Is it all right . . ." His voice petered out, like he lost his courage halfway through his sentence, and he cleared his throat. "Is it all right if we don't do anything yet?"

I twisted around to look at him. "Do any of what thing?"

"You know. I haven't done *this*." He squeezed my hand, but when I went on staring blankly, he sighed, nose crinkling with embarrassment. "I've never *been* with anyone before."

"Oh. Oh!" I rolled over onto my back so our twined hands rested upon my stomach. "Really?"

"Don't sound so surprised."

"I *am* surprised. Frankly, I'm shocked. You didn't strike me as pure and chaste when you pinned me up against that wall in Venice."

"Oh God." Percy covered his face with his free hand.

"Or Paris, when you climbed right onto my lap—"

"Stop it."

"—and knew exactly where to put your—"

"I'm not *entirely* ignorant." He jabbed me in the ribs again. "Just because I'm a . . . virgin . . ." He tripped over the word, and somehow that alone was enough for all the blood to leave my head. I could feel his skin going hot against mine as he blushed. "Doesn't mean I haven't . . . I mean, I've got the same . . . you know . . . bits . . . as you so I've had some . . . practice on . . . Oh my God, is this *working* for you?"

"I'm sorry!" I tugged my nightshirt down between my legs, though it did little to hide the fact that yes, inexplicably, it really was.

He snorted, his neck arching against the pillow. "Dear Lord, you're incorrigible."

"You're just so adorable when you're flustered!" I pulled up my knees and did my best to make a fig leaf of my hands. I couldn't stop laughing, though the pitch made *giggling* the far more appropriate term. "And you're half naked in bed with me," I added. "That does wonders for the circulation."

He rubbed his hands over his face with a rueful

smile, like he was trying to wipe away the color in his cheeks. "Is it really so strange to think I've gone this long without it?"

"No, no," I said quickly. "It's more that I find it hard to understand how every single person you meet doesn't want to climb you like a ladder."

He laughed, his eyes flitting downward so his lashes cast thin shadows upon his cheeks. "Yes, well, I've been rather occupied for most of my life with wanting only you."

"Oh, Perce." I touched my forehead to his. "You're so monogamous."

"Come here." He hooked his leg around mine, both of us so dewy with the heat that our skin met with a very unromantic squelch, then buried his face in my shoulder so his words came out muffled. "Is that all right? If we hold off for a bit on any . . ."

"Deflowering?"

"In a word."

"'Course it's all right. Percy, *of course*."

"Really?"

"Did you think that it wouldn't be?"

"I don't know. I'm new to all this, and you're so very

not." That last bit stung, though I wasn't certain why, for it was true. When I didn't say anything, he added, "I'm not as handsome as you, remember? People don't throw themselves at me."

"*I've* been throwing myself at you for years," I said. "It's your own damn fault you never noticed."

He raised his head, and I leaned in for a kiss, a momentary stutter in the action borne from years of holding back every time I was close to him. He hooked a finger in the neck of my shirt, pulling me to him, and what I had intended to be a light peck turned open-mouthed and deep-breathed.

Until I pulled away. Reluctantly. "I thought you wanted to hold off."

"Well." A crease appeared between his eyebrows, and I loved how disappointed he looked by our kiss cut short. "We don't have to keep our hands entirely to ourselves."

I laughed, and he settled down against me so that his palm cupped my rib cage, fingertips against my heartbeat. We both fell asleep before it went any further than that, exhausted from the sun and the water and rolling around in sand and mutual adoration all afternoon.

Supremely chaste in all but thought.

And less chaste the next morning, after he left me alone. It's maddening that Percy's and my fondness has finally been acknowledged as mutual and yet I'm keeping myself company like I'm fourteen years old again. Though at fourteen, I could not have imagined this flat or this summer we'd had, or that a life outside my father's house was about to unfurl like a carpet at my feet.

Or the growing dread that the first step I took upon it, I'd fall hard on my face, and Percy would leave me behind.

THREE

Felicity executes her plan to get Percy and me alone, naked, and horizontal as unsubtly as possible: by announcing it over breakfast.

"I think we should have a party away from the flat."

Scipio and Ebrahim, both taking the meal with us, look up from their food in almost comical unison. Scipio sets his knife across his plate, then says, "That seems . . . out of character for you to request."

Felicity presses on with unnecessary zeal. "I was doing some reading, and it's Assumption Day this week, and most places on the island will be closed for the festivities. So I don't think there's any point in you working on the *Eleftheria* that day. Also you've made tremendous progress on the repairs and the cargo is all off-loaded and we'll be off soon so why not have a bit of a gathering? And also my birthday is coming up."

"That"—I press my toe into her shin under the table and give her a pointed look—"is too many reasons."

Ebrahim spears a half a fig and looks to his captain. "We're due for a night off. The crew has been working hard. We could go into Finikia for some food and cards. They've got good bars there." My first reaction is wanting to go along before I remember the whole thing is a ploy I am not allowed to partake in. Though he didn't have to make it so goddamn exciting.

"I thought your birthday was in March," Percy says suddenly to Felicity.

She shakes her head with far too much enthusiasm. It looks like a stage pantomime meant to be seen from the galleries. "No, you must be remembering wrong," she says, then adds in a great rush, "Monty, would you and Percy go fetch the teapot and cups? I left them beside the stove."

Percy is still entirely focused on some sort of complex calendar math as I take him by the arm and drag him after me into the kitchen before either he exposes Felicity's lie or Felicity does that herself. As soon as we're out of earshot, I knock his knee with my foot—my hands being occupied with gathering up mismatched mugs for tea—to get him to pay attention to me. "I have a proposition for you."

"Am I wrong?" he asks, looking up from emptying the steaming kettle into the teapot.

"About what?"

"Felicity's birthday is in March, isn't it? Because it fell on Easter one year, and you told her Jesus would be angry at her for stealing his day."

"Yes, well, that's related to my proposition."

"Jesus being angry at your sister?"

"No, the overly elaborate lie she just told to make sure the flat would be empty for us."

"Oh." Realization dawns suddenly and a splash of hot water misses the pot. "Oh!"

"Yes." I resist an eyebrow wiggle. "*Oh*."

"You . . ." He looks down at the kettle, then back up at me. "Set a date for it."

I did, didn't I? That put rather a lot of emphasis on the affair, not to mention a very intimidating countdown. My stomach flips unpleasantly. "Only if you're ready," I say quickly. "Sorry, I should have asked. We could go out with the crew instead. Or go out on our own and eat a lot of cakes. Or stay here and lie next to each other in rigid silence without touching until—"

"Yes," he interrupts.

I pause. "Yes to which of those?"

"Yes, I would like to stay in with you for the very specific reasons for which you designed this deception," he says. "As upsetting as I find it that Felicity is involved."

"Hardly involved." He raises an eyebrow, and I add, "I was desperate."

"Yes, I should hope she wasn't your first choice." He takes up the pitcher, then leans forward and kisses me on the temple, and I will never not be simultaneously infuriated and amused and a tiny bit aroused by our vast height difference. Though lately Percy could sneeze and I'd be sporting a partial. "Thank you for being patient with me."

It's less about being patient and more simply about getting myself off for the last several weeks, but saying that will likely come off rather less romantic than I intend, so instead I reply, "I'm very good at patience," and am only a tiny bit resentful when he laughs.

When we return to the table with the tea, Georgie has joined us, sitting on the ledge of the garden path and happily demolishing a handful of honeycomb. When he sees Percy, he scoots down to sit beside him.

"I brought a letter for you," Georgie says to Percy.

"A letter?" Percy repeats. "From you?"

"Are you writing Percy love letters, Georgie?" I tease. Georgie is, in a word, obsessed with Percy. I'd be jealous if Georgie weren't ten years old and his devotion to Percy so damn adorable.

"From London." Georgie reaches into his trousers—not my favorite place for him to be carrying things he's bringing us—and withdraws a folded sheet of parchment with a London port-of-origin stamp, which he hands to Percy.

Percy's face sobers as he breaks the seal. "It's from my uncle." His eyes scan the page, and we all sit, watching him read and waiting to hear the verdict. Scipio leans forward at the table, hands flat against each other and pressed to his lips. I'm not sure he means to, but he looks as though he's praying.

Percy had written to his uncle at the same time Felicity and I had written to inform our parents we wouldn't be coming home. Percy's tone had been far more gentle, both because his request required some delicacy and because Percy is less of a battering ram incarnate than my sister and me. His plea had been that his uncle use his position on the admiralty court in Cheshire to grant the crew of the *Eleftheria*—a crew, Percy had reminded him, that he was already acquainted with and whom he respected—a letter of marque allowing them to sail legitimately in the service of the English crown as thanks for our rescue. We had expected to have quit the island before Thomas Powell's reply could reach us. Percy's letter had been meant as notice that Scipio and his men would request a meeting with him when they arrived in England and that it should be granted, as they had done the three of us a great service. But the delay in our return had apparently given him enough time to write back to us. Had that been anticipated, I suspect Percy wouldn't have included a paragraph about his own plans for his future, namely that he would not be going to the asylum in Holland his aunt and uncle had arranged for him.

"He says he remembers you," Percy says to Scipio and Ebrahim. "And he's happy to see a letter of marque issued, and for such fine sailors to join the ranks of the

English fleet—look here, those are his exact words." As Scipio peers at the letter over his shoulder, Percy's eyes flick to mine, then he reads, "'And though your aunt and I do not feel we can support a life for you beyond institutionalization, your choice lies outside our control. We can only trust that you have made the necessary accommodations for your own health as well as the comfort of those around you.'" He winces on the final words, and in spite of how much good news he delivered, I'm ready to sail to England that minute to challenge Thomas Powell to a duel for the way he writes of Percy's epilepsy, like it's a burden to others.

But then Percy looks up at me. "All right. That's not bad."

Felicity and I trade a glance. "He won't tell our parents, you think?" she asks.

"I didn't mention where we are," Percy said. "Or where we'll be going. Or that I'm still with the two of you. Besides, he doesn't particularly care for your father."

I keep my mouth shut. Best not to mention the letter I had sent to Father, which had single-handedly revealed all this information as a means of delivering a cross-continent Agincourt salute. In my defense, I wouldn't have written it had I not been certain he would not lift a finger after me, or had I not had iron-clad collateral to keep him away. In spite of what my sister may think, I do think things through. Sometimes. Most things. But I'd rather not have that called into question just now.

Scipio leans back in his chair with a faint smile. I suspect he's trying to hide how relieved he is that taking us three on was not entirely for naught. "That's good news."

"His office is in Liverpool," Percy continues, still studying the letter. "He wants you to come there and meet with him as soon as you make port."

"And will you come with us?" Scipio asks.

"To Liverpool?" Percy folds the letter and passes it to Felicity, who is holding out an expectant hand. "Not likely. I thought London instead."

"London?" I repeat. This was the first I'd heard of it.

He looks over at me. "We talked about London, didn't we? I assumed that's where we'd go."

"What about . . ." I give a vague wave at the courtyard around us, suddenly feeling very attached to everything about this island. Breath-stealing hills and roaches included.

"It doesn't seem practical to live outside of England—we'll get on much better without having to worry about foreign documentation," he replies. "And we both speak the language—your French isn't good enough to set up anywhere else. And I thought it would be a decent place for me to find work. Try to get a post as a music teacher, or a hired musician."

"You have . . ." I stare down at the surface of my tea. "Given this quite a lot of thought."

"Haven't you?" Felicity asks. I glare at her. It's not her fault I haven't looked beyond our time in the Cyclades, but she could be a little less obnoxiously shocked by it.

"Where will you be going, Miss Montague?" Scipio asks, and I'm prepared to offer her an equally smug condemnation of her lack of preparedness, but before I can, she says with great conviction, "To Edinburgh."

"You won't be signing on with us, then?" Scipio asks, though he sounds as if he already knows the answer.

Felicity swipes the corner of her mouth with her napkin. "Your offer of a position with your crew is very considerate, but I can't see being a ship surgeon as a truly viable career for me. I'd like more than anything to

get a medical education and receive some formal school-
ing in the subject. And since Edinburgh has the best
hospitals in the country and the only university offering
medical degrees, I'm going there."

"You think the university will let you in?" I ask,
pouncing upon my first opportunity to pick holes in her
plan. "Or are you going to start wearing breeches like a
boy and hope no one notices your hairless chin?"

"What are you going to do in London?" she counters.
"Strangely, I can't see any of your skills being monetized.
Aside from one, though I think they prefer ladies for
that."

"Don't be mean," I snap, then take a very, very long
drink of tea that is far too hot to be drunk, particularly for that long, in hopes that if I stall enough they'll
move the conversation forward without me. I am apparently the only one who has avoided thinking about what
happens once we leave the island, or neglected to even
realize the future required a plan. And the list of my particular skills has been thoroughly exhausted in the last
month: sunbathing and sleeping late and looking handsome while eating grapes.

Scipio passes Georgie a napkin for his sticky hands,

which he instead uses to blow his nose and then returns. "With the assurance of a letter of marque, we'll want to be off soon," Scipio says. "As soon as possible. The last payment is due next week and the repairs should be finished as well."

"All the more reason for a party," Felicity says, and looks at me again, this time with a different but equally obvious weight.

"Why not?" Scipio says. "There's much to celebrate."

Under the table, Percy puts his hand on my knee and squeezes. I take another drink of tea and wish it was something stronger.

FOUR

Since Felicity prepared the breakfast, Percy and I clean up—him washing the dishes and me drying. My head is hurting in a way that I'm not entirely certain can be blamed on my recent injury, but I'm entirely certain I'm going to blame it anyway in order to justify going back to bed.

"We should probably discuss it," Percy says as he hands me a plate.

"Discuss what?"

"London. What we'll do when we get there."

"Oh right. That." I scrape at a bit of food stuck to the dish with my fingernail. "It'll all work itself out."

Percy frowns. "Well. No. We need some kind of plan."

"Why? It's London." I add the dry plate to the stack and take the next one he offers me. "I know London."

"You know the Covent Garden club scene."

"Is that not helpful?"

He gives me a look that clearly conveys we are not yet to the point of joking about the purchasable companionship I have previously enjoyed in our capital, and I drop my grin.

"Well, where are we going to live?" he asks.

"In London."

"Stop it, you're annoying me." He flicks a handful of suds at me. "I mean *where*?"

"I dunno. In a house."

"We can't afford a house."

Now it's my turn to frown. "Can't we?"

"We probably can't even afford a flat for a while."

My hand slips on the plate I'm drying. It shatters on the floor between us, and we both jump backward to avoid the shards. "Damn it."

I start to bend down, just as Percy says, "Don't worry, it's only—watch out, you're going to cut yourself." He throws out a cautioning hand to me, and I freeze.

"Goddammit, sorry—"

"It's fine. Just be careful."

"You too."

"I've shoes on; you haven't."

Percy takes a knee, collecting the largest shards in a pile, while I remain obediently and impotently frozen until he says, "Hand me the broom, won't you?"

I do the requested broom handing, then, useless again, watch him sweep up the mess I made. "I can finish the dishes on my own," I offer as he tosses the broken plate into our rubbish bin.

He dusts his hands off on his trousers. "Don't be a martyr—it'll only take a few minutes more. Just be careful with these," he adds as he picks up the knife set, and I feel like a scolded child. After a moment of thoughtful scrubbing at a spot on the blade, Percy says, "We don't have to talk about London right now. But think on it, all right? I'd prefer if we leave here with some sort of strategy." He leans toward me, pressing our shoulders together. "And until then, I am looking forward to Felicity's birthday."

"Oh. Yes."

"Start things off right."

I almost drop another piece of dishware. "What do you mean *start*?"

"Going to London will be the start, won't it? Start of all this. Living together and on our own and being . . . you know. Partnered." When I don't say anything, he prompts in a tone that is trying too hard to be casual, "You are still coming with me, aren't you?"

"Yes, of course."

He glances over at me. "Then it's a start."

"Right."

"A new beginning."

"Right."

"I think that's dry."

"Right. What?" I look down at the glass in my hand—I've rubbed its insides raw with the towel. I set it down, and it lands with such a hard clatter I worry for a moment I've broken it too. Percy looks sideways at me, then passes over a handful of cutlery.

We finish the rest in silence.

FIVE

On the appointed night, Percy and I go down to the beach for dinner with the crew, but as the sun begins to set and everyone else heads to Finikia, we turn in. We make the long climb up the cliffside and through the crumbling stucco labyrinth of Oia back to our flat. In the darkness, the cobalt domes look dark as India ink. When I start to moan about my legs being tired, Percy consents to carry me on his back the rest of the way to the flat. I lean my chin on his shoulder and use the darkness as an excuse to trace the shape of his ear with my tongue, then down his neck.

"If you keep doing that," he says, "I'm going to put you down."

"Why?" I bite down gently on his lobe. "Am I getting you excited?"

"No, you're getting yourself excited, and it's not particularly comfortable for me."

I laugh, and the familiar flirtation settles the nerves that had been sitting like stones in the pit of my stomach since morning.

It's just Percy, I remind myself. *It's just you and Percy and nothing to be anxious about.*

I slide off his back at the top of the hill, and we walk into the courtyard together. Percy stops dead on the walk, surveying the ridiculous display of candles and flowers and food and three bottles of wine, which seems excessive, even to me. And a tad insulting. Like we're going to need that much liquid courage to get things going.

It is . . . a lot. More than I expected it to be. Felicity had told me she would get some flowers and lay them out clandestinely after Percy and I went down to the beach. But this is quite a bit more than we discussed. Or perhaps she had discussed it and I hadn't been listening. My stomach drops.

"What's all this?" Percy asks me.

"Oh, you know." I give a vague wave at it, like it's hardly worth mentioning. "Ambivalence."

He looks sideways at me. "What?"

"It was Felicity's idea. She said I should create ambivalence."

A pause. Percy's face is screwed up in thought. I suddenly feel hot and sticky all over, too aware of every place where my clothes sit upon my body and desperate to itch them all.

"Ambiance," he says suddenly.

"What?"

"Ambiance. That's what you meant. Not ambivalence."

"Right. Yes, that."

"Well, well done, Felicity. And you, obviously." Percy reaches for a tray and plucks one of the aniseed pastries he's eaten his weight in since we arrived. "All this for me?"

"Yes. Well, except I know you don't like figs as much as I do, so I suppose those are for me." He's already finished his second pastry and is moving in for a third. I bat his hand out of the air. "Stop eating them."

"I thought they were for me."

"Yes, but listen to me first." I grab his hands between us, then take a deep breath. "Percy."

"Monty." His eyes flit over my shoulder to the tray. Dear Lord, I am sincerely competing with food for his attention? Am I doing that poorly already? "May I have another pastry while you talk? Or are you going to give me something else to do with my mouth?"

"I mean . . . not no." I swallow hard, my throat suddenly dry. Am I supposed to say something here? Something romantic and sweet and not maudlin? Hadn't I planned something to say? If I had, I can't remember it now. Dear God, why did I agree to make a production of this? We should have gotten this big first over unceremoniously, with no pastries and no flowers and no speeches, though I wouldn't say no to a bit of wine. Why is it so much easier to take my trousers off in front of someone I couldn't give a fig about?

"This doesn't change anything, does it?" I blurt.

Percy cocks his head. "Really? That's what you want to lead with?"

"That's not what I . . . I just mean . . ." I reach up to scratch at the scars around my missing ear, but he catches my hand before I can. I let out a shaky breath.

"You want to do this?" I say. "With me?"

"I do."

"You're certain?"

"'Course I'm certain." He weaves his fingers between mine and kisses my knuckles. "Why? Don't you want to?"

"No."

"No?" He goes absolutely still, like an animal who has heard the first snapping twig beneath a hunter's boot.

"No. Wait. I mean, yes, I want to. Sorry, I thought you were going to ask . . ." Dear Lord, perhaps three bottles of wine isn't enough. "Yes. Of course, yes."

"All right."

"All right."

And then we just look at each other.

And not in the romantic *we're about to kiss* sort of way. It's more of the *what now* variety. Not the gaze you hope will preface a passionate embrace.

"Should we . . ." I start right as he leans in to kiss me.

And then we both stop. So now we are uncomfortably looking at each other from an inch apart. Which is worse. And then I start talking again right as he leans in. Again.

But Percy laughs as he straightens. "You go first."

"I was just . . . do you want to go into the bedroom?" I regret it as soon as I say it. It makes me uncomfortably aware of how desperate I am to get this over with, and how little sense that makes. I have never in all my born days been this clumsy about getting tangled up with someone. Perhaps it's because it's Percy, the first person with whom I've ever made it this far that mattered. Or perhaps it's because in the shadowy corners of my heart, I know I'm the sort of person you romp with for one wild night and then you climb out the window before I wake. The sort of person no one wants to be around unless there's some kind of reward involved, preferably of a sexual nature. Not the sort you bet all your chips on a life with. How long before he realizes that? And how much longer before he regrets wasting his first time on me?

"Bedroom," I say again, and somehow it lands with even more of a clunk than before. "Yes. Let's do that."

"All right."

No, wait, not yet! Stall! my brain screams at me, and

I only make it a step before I skid to an involuntary halt. "Or." I pivot to face Percy again. "Or maybe we just stay here and have a drink?"

He smiles, and my throat closes. "That's good too."

And then I reach for the wine, and my brain screams at me again. *No, don't drag this out, get it over with! Having a drink in awkward pre-fornication silence will not make this better! But also don't go to the bedroom!*

And I stop. Again. With no idea what to do next.

My brain is an arsehole.

"Actually." I pause. "Yes. Upstairs."

"Upstairs?" he repeats, and I realize I am still, confusingly, reaching for the wine.

"Yes." I fumble around and catch his hand, like that was my intention all along. I'm shakier than I thought I would be, and I immediately wish I hadn't touched him. My limbs feel like they're made of smoke. Very panicked smoke. "Bedroom. Upstairs."

Good, I've been reduced to single-word sentences. That will certainly turn him on.

I lead Percy up the stairs to the small room I've claimed on the second floor, blessing the narrow hallways that require us to walk single file if we still want to hold hands because it means I don't have to look him in the eye yet.

I stop dead in the doorway of my bedroom, like I smacked into a sheet of glass, because suddenly everything about this room seems to proclaim, *This is the place where you have sex and start your life together! It all begins here! THIS IS THE FIRST PLACE YOU WILL DISAPPOINT THE PERSON YOU LOVE!*

I feel Percy stop behind me, then he says, "I'm disappointed."

Which is so aggressively in tune with my panicked internal monologue that I swear I almost faint. "What? Why?"

"I thought there'd be more pastries."

"Oh God." I lean backward against him, bumping his chest with my shoulders. "You and your disgusting pastries. They're not good, you know."

"I know." He wraps his arms around my waist and presses his lips to my neck. *I can do this,* I tell myself. *I can do this, I'm fine, I can do this.* "But I can't stop eating them."

"They're hard as rocks. You're going to break a tooth."

"Would you still find me handsome if I broke my teeth on Greek pastries?"

"Depends which teeth."

"Too late. You're stuck with me."

He leans over my shoulder to kiss me. But without meaning to, I duck away from it, which is unexpected. For both of us. Percy freezes, still for a moment, then his hands start to fall away from my waist.

"Are you sure this is safe?" I blurt out. It's the first thing that comes to my mind.

And it's not excellent.

I turn to him as he quirks an eyebrow. "Safe?"

"For you. I mean. It's not going to cause a fit or anything?"

Thank God he laughs at this. Though less in a *how funny* way. It rings more with *are you truly this stupid?* Or perhaps that's just me assigning subterranean levels to every goddamn breath he takes. "I know I'm new at this, but I'm fairly confident no doctor has ever confirmed that losing your virginity can cause an epileptic fit."

"Just . . ." I bite the inside of my cheek. "Thought I'd ask."

I must look cowed, for his face softens. He steps into the room in front of me and takes my face in both his hands. "What's wrong?"

"Nothing's wrong."

"You're acting strange."

"I'm not."

"We don't have to do this."

"No, I want to. I'm sorry, I'll do better."

"There's nothing to do better. Just . . . promise you'd tell me if you were bothered about something?"

"I promise."

Too late! says my arsehole brain.

I lean up to kiss him, as though that proves how not-strange I am acting, and wait for the calm that always comes from touching Percy to settle through me. But it has left the building. Instead I'm stiff and tense and so aware of how awkward it is to have someone's lips smashed against yours. It's like I've forgotten how to kiss him. How to kiss anyone. I can't make my mouth open, even as his tongue prods my teeth. I have no idea what to do with my hands. What do people do with their hands when they kiss? Surely they don't simply let them hang like limp vines at their sides, which is what I'm doing now.

I take hold of . . . his elbow. Which is somehow less romantic than not touching him at all. He seems to agree, for, with our mouths still together, he does a very careful extrication of said elbow from my grip, which leaves me pawing at the air again like I'm treading water. He reaches up and cups my face in his hands, so gentle and so sweet, and why does someone as gentle and sweet as Percy Newton want to be with someone as raw and rough as me?

We stay like that for a while, soft and tame and completely within the same boundaries we've skirted for the past weeks, and it's going to be fine, I tell myself. Everything is going to be fine and my heart is not about to punch its way through my rib cage, and it's Percy and it's fine, it's fine, it's so goddamn fine and could not be finer.

Percy is either oblivious to the fact that this is not usually the sort of fond touching that preludes fornication, or he's pretending he hasn't noticed I'm losing my goddamn mind, for he wraps his arms around my

61

waist and pulls me up against him. Which is mortifying because, for perhaps the first time I've been in Percy's presence, since I was fifteen years old, my arms are not the only things hanging limp.

He either can feel me tense or feels just how not tense an essential area pressed against him is, because he stops suddenly and looks down at me with his brow creased. "Am I doing something wrong?" he asks.

"No," I say, and somehow it comes out both hoarse and shrill at the same time, like a songbird that has smoked too many cigars.

"You're shaking. Are you all right?"

"I'm fine." In an attempt to stall for time, I drag out the word *fine* for so long that I run out of air. Percy blinks at me, for I am clearly not fine but still clinging to the slim chance that I might have him fooled. "Let's sit."

"Sit?"

"On the bed." Like somehow that will help anything, but he follows my lead and we sit. On the bed. Side by side. Not touching.

I scrub at my hair. Percy looks up at the ceiling. Loud, slow seconds tick by, each one a stone dropped onto my chest. I'm going to be pressed to death like a witch, except instead of boulders it will be the weight of my own goddamn issues that kills me.

Before I can obsess a moment longer, I lunge over and kiss him again, fast and graceless. Our teeth knock. It feels like a stage kiss, two passionless actors, and poor, darling Percy who expected me to take him by the hand and lead him into this garden of earthly delights is instead left stumbling blind and alone in the dark, knocking over furniture and smashing into walls.

And then he pulls away from me, puts his hands in his lap, and asks bluntly, "Do you not want me?"

It's the worst thing anyone has ever said to me. First because it is so fantastically untrue but I have no evidence, physical or otherwise, to support my denial, and second because I can see in the hurt on his face that he's thinking of every time he walked in on me with my hands up some girl's skirt in the side room off a party, and now here we are, alone at last after me making declaration after declaration that I kept company with unwavering love for him during all those hands-up-skirts years and yet I'm acting as though I'm getting warmed up to do it with an upturned mop wearing a wig.

He's hurt. And mortified. I'm similarly mortified

and trying to work out how it is that I've been burning off absurd amounts of energy waiting for exactly this moment with exactly him and now that the appointed hour has arrived—all this planning and overture and dear Lord, there were *figs*—we're three feet apart, staring at each other like we're strangers.

And then I say, "I'm sorry," before I realize that I didn't answer his question about whether I wanted him, so it sounds like I'm apologizing for not wanting him, and Lord I have never felt more like a pile of soggy porridge molded into human form. "Wait, no, that's not . . ."

He looks down at his hands, those fine, long fingers that I want to snatch back and press against my heart, but I can't move. "It's fine," he says, and he sounds almost as not-fine as I feel.

"That's not what I meant."

"But something's wrong."

"Nothing's wrong."

He turns, one leg pulled up under him on the bed so he's properly facing me. "Monty."

My eyes dart around the room. "I really, really want to."

"All right, so . . ." He tips his head like he's going to

kiss me, and I lean back without thinking and dear God I almost let myself fall off the bed in hopes I will strike my head and in the resulting blackout, lose all memory that this ever happened. Perhaps I should drag Percy down after me, just to make certain we both forget.

He pulls back, sucking in his cheeks hard, and I swear I hear him curse under his breath.

Shame curls inside of me, but I take a breath, trying to fight through it and explain myself, though I still can't work out what the hell is happening to me. "This is important to you," I say.

"Isn't it important to you?" he says, his voice snappish.

"Well, I mean . . ." He raises an eyebrow, an unmistakable *tread carefully*, and so of course I put on my heaviest boots and start clomping through the flower gardens. "Yes, but . . . it's not like it's anything . . . remarkable . . . sex is actually . . . it's a part of nature, so it's really not . . . worms do it, you know."

Percy squints at me, and I look around for something sharp I can impale myself upon. Better to fall on my sword now than prolong this slow death.

"Worms?" Percy repeats.

"I just don't think it should be some kind of grand affair," I say, too fast and too loud. "And if you're going to make it one, I think we should wait."

"I'm not making it—"

"You kept saying how it was your first—"

"I did not," he interrupts sharply.

"You did!"

"Well you're the one who filled up our courtyard with flowers and figs."

"That was Felicity's ambivalence!"

"Ambiance!"

I throw up my hands. "I don't care!"

Percy looks away from me, his mouth tight. "God, you're such a . . ."

He trails off, and I feel my chin rise in defiance. "Excuse me?"

"I didn't say anything."

"Yes you did. I'm such a what, Percy? Go on, say it."

"You're such a prick!" he bursts out. "I was *so* excited about this and now you're being a prick and ruining it."

I clench my hands into fists around the loose material of my trousers. "Then maybe we shouldn't. Since I'm such a prick." He looks away from me, and I'm sure he'll take it back, but when he doesn't, I press on, "We've been doing fine without it—*I'm* doing fine—and if this will change everything, then maybe it's better if we don't do it. Now. Or ever. Maybe ever. Maybe things should just stay the way they are."

I can tell he's trying to follow that unmappable logic, made all the more inscrutable by how dedicated I am to both my nonsense and how violently I have just vomited it onto him. Then he says slowly, "So you don't want to do this anymore?"

"Not until you figure out—"

"Me?" he snaps. "How is any of this my fault?"

"Because you had to make it out to be some sort of life-changing event, and it's not!" I burst out. It's not fair that I'm doing this to him, making it seem like it's him keeping us apart when it is so obviously not. I know I'm being cruel and selfish, the two things I had very recently promised him I would try to be less of, but either old habits die with as much collateral damage as possible, or maybe this is just who I am. Maybe I can't separate myself from the spite that sent me ducking before my father's hand for years—it's sewn into my blood like choking weeds. "Maybe this isn't a good idea. I don't think you're ready."

"Fine." He looks away from me, his jaw set. "Maybe we're not."

"It's not me."

"It sort of feels like it is."

"Well, you're wrong, and it's not." I stand up and head defiantly for the door. I'm halfway through my storm-out when I realize this is *my* room I'm storming out of. My steps stutter, and I consider pressing on just because I'm already neck deep in this, might as well go under. I could kip up in his room to deliver the mental flogging I'm about to unleash upon myself, but the sheets will smell of him and his clothes will be on the floor and the mattress will be caved to the shape of his body and somehow that will make it all so much worse.

So instead I stop, and I turn on him—both literally and figuratively. "Could you just leave? Please?"

And he does. He doesn't touch me, or even look at me on his way out, nor does he stop in the doorway for a look back. I hadn't realized how desperately I hoped he would until he doesn't. He leaves. Full stop. And I lie down on my own bed, alone and marinating in shame. What should have been our first night sleeping together is another night of me sleeping alone.

When the crew comes back to the flat for one last round, I'm still awake. They're rowdy with drinking and their voices float up from the courtyard, someone telling a story with so much oblivious joy, about a mermaid, it makes me sick with jealousy. I had thought about going down to clean up the flotsam of our failed night, but I didn't have the strength. Either Percy must have faced it for me or it's all still there and the crew is simply too up in their altitudes to make sense of the drooping flowers and still-corked wine.

Felicity must notice. I hear her light steps on the stairs, then they pause outside my door. She's likely expecting to hear, if not the sounds of active sodomy, at least two sets of snores. She stands there for so long I think she might knock, which would be literally the only thing that could make this night worse. But instead, I hear her retreat, the door to her room shutting very quietly, and we all sleep alone.

SIX

When I wake the next morning, the first thing I think of is how badly I want a finger of whiskey.

The second is whether I can go this whole day in this tiny house on this tiny island without having to see Percy.

The third thing I think of is whiskey again, but more than a finger. And then scotch. And claret and rum and literally any goddamn thing I could pour down my throat that will make it possible to think about something other than how badly I've mucked everything up between us. I consider waking Felicity to ask for her advice, then I realize there's no advice she can give me because I've already done the stupid thing. I want a drink so bad I'm trembling, and since I've ruined things with Percy, what's the point of sobriety and being a changed man? I get up, yank on my trousers, and go downstairs to find spirits.

The house is hot and quiet—and after a night of wild revelry among some parties and intense self-loathing among others, I'm not certain who ended up kipping up here or, more important, who might be awake and prowling. The kitchen is blessedly empty when I arrive and start rooting around for some sort of libations—any and all varieties welcome, large quantities preferred. I would have cut off my left testicle, which I can't help but think I'll no longer be needing, for even a swallow of the toxic gin served in Covent Garden theaters. My head is pounding.

A door opens upstairs, and my desperation for a drink is trumped by my fear of that door belonging to Percy's room. I'm not sure which I want to do less—make awkward breakfast talk with him like nothing happened or have an actual discussion—so I choose neither and instead flee the kitchen empty-handed. I let myself out the back door, then take the path behind the flat that leads to the cliffs where the crew likes to dive. The rocky outcropping overlooks the ocean, rippling green and silver in turn as the sunlight catches the seaweed below the surface, then the break of the waves. I sit down on a shaggy rock near the edge and press the toes of my slippers into the soft sand. The morning is already stupidly hot and the water aggravatingly pretty, and I don't have any idea how long I can hide here before I face the fact that Percy wants things to start, and I am just not stable enough for that, and may never be. Though perhaps that whole point of starting something together is moot because I was such an embarrassing mess last night that he'll never want to be near me again.

My hiding works for approximately five minutes. Maybe less. Primarily because, I realize as I hear the path behind me crunching underfoot, this cliffside perch is incredibly visible from most windows of the flat.

"Oh no." I pull my knees up to my chest and bury my face in my arms when Percy sits down next to me, his breath coming out in a huff. "Don't look at me. I'm hideous."

"Oh stop. You know you're gorgeous." I hear the scratch of him rubbing his fingers through his hair, then he lets out another heavy sigh. "So. Last night."

I keep my forehead pressed into my arms. "Please don't make me talk about it. I hate talking about my feelings."

"Please. You have more feelings more vocally than any human on this earth." His shoulder knocks into mine once, then he presses it there until I consent to look up at him. He's wound his hair back into a messy knot, and the morning sun streaks it with liquid gold. He looks tired. I'm sure I do as well. We might not have slept together, but at least we were sleepless together.

"So what happened?" he asks. "Because perhaps I was imagining things, but you seemed aggressively less interested in me last night than usual. Or . . . ever."

"Lies. I am incredibly interested in you always."

"You gave me the distinct impression otherwise." I drop my head again with a moan. "Sorry," he says quickly, "I shouldn't have said that. Will you please tell me what I did wrong?"

"Nothing!" My head shoots up. "God, no, not at all, it's not you."

"You seemed to think it was last night."

"Yes, well. I was not my best self last night."

"Neither was I."

I let out a hollow laugh. "No, no, you were, as always, a perfect gentleman."

"I wasn't. And I should have stopped and forced you

to have a proper conversation instead of letting myself believe you when you said everything was fine when it clearly wasn't. And I shouldn't have snapped at you."

Had any of that happened? I had been so self-obsessed I hadn't noticed. "Those still sound more like *my* problems than yours."

"But I should have thought of you more. I've been so focused on whether or not *I* was ready that it never occurred to me that you might not be. And you're not a prick," he adds. "You were a bit last night, but most days you're not."

I snort. "Thank you?"

"I'm sorry I called you a prick. That's what I'm trying to say. I'm sorry." There's silence for a moment, in which I sincerely contemplate how badly I would like the ground to open and swallow me whole. Then he prompts, "Your turn."

I rub my hands across my face. "Can we talk about this later?"

"No."

"I'm so tired."

"So am I. Tell me what's wrong."

"I don't know!" I say it so loud that a gull takes flight

from where it's pecking about the seagrass sprouting up between the rocks. "I just can't get my head on straight."

He hesitates, then asks, "Can you give me a bit more than that?"

He glances at my hands, clasped so hard between my knees my knuckles are white. "Are you all right? You're trembling."

I shove my hands under my thighs and will them to still. "I'm fine," I say out of habit. When Percy keeps staring at me, I add, "I really want a drink. And I really wish I didn't." The truth surprises me. I had been reaching for a lie but spoken before I could find one. This mutinous brain of mine. I stare out at the water, letting the salt sting my eyes, and laugh without meaning to. "I'm so pathetic."

"You're not pathetic," Percy says. "I think they were drinking at the flat last night, but I can make certain all the spirits have been cleared out."

I look over at him, the lines of his face made fuzzy by the sun, and my heart strains in my chest. How had loving him this much made me selfish and drunk and awful, while he had grown even kinder and softer in its harsh light?

"I'll be all right."

"I know you will be," he says. "But you don't have to do it alone." He reaches out and squeezes my arm, a quick touch that is still miles from the sort of fondness we've shared in the past few weeks.

I take a breath and remind myself: I am not alone in any of this.

"Do you need something to eat?" he asks. "Or I could fetch you some tea or—"

"No," I interrupt him. "Let's talk. I want to talk." I scrub a hand over my chin, wishing I'd shaved. "I'm not certain how to explain it. But love and sex have been separate things for me for so long because they had to be," I say. "I was almost always with someone because I was bored and hated myself, and it was something to do that wasn't thinking about either of those things. I've never been with anyone because I loved them and wanted something more together. So this has never required any sort of emotional component, and I don't know how to do that. I don't even know if I can. Maybe I'm too far gone."

"I don't believe that for an instant." He folds his arms around his knees. "Look how far you've come already."

"But what about in six months," I say, "when I've got no job and I've wrecked my sobriety and I'm mean to you and won't get out of bed and you can't stand to be around me?"

He tips his head backward, the ghost of a smile passing over his lips. "So this *is* about London."

"No," I say defensively, then add, "What about London?"

"When I started talking about where we were going next at breakfast the other morning, I had a sense you were panicking."

"Well, I wasn't *then*."

"Retroactive panic counts."

I press my fingernails hard into my scalp, the heels of my hands against my eyes. "Maybe I was panicking. Maybe I am. Because I just don't think I can do it, Perce." My voice breaks, and I swallow hard. "I don't think I'm good enough for you. And I don't want you to do this big thing—give me this big part of yourself—and then realize you made a mistake."

We sit in silence for a long time. Down the hill, I hear pottery shatter against tile. Someone laughs. A pair of gulls above us snaps at each other with a shriek.

Then Percy asks, "Who was your first?"

"What?"

He gives me a very deliberate look.

"Oh. That."

"I can't remember you ever having a first time; you were just suddenly swaggering and confident about it."

"Yes, well, I'm very swaggery."

He refuses to fall for the diversion, and instead digs his elbow into my side. "So?"

I sigh. "Amelia Wickham. Do you remember her? She was older than us—ran off to Gretna Green with Geoffrey Holland last summer. Had a lot of freckles and always talked about how much she hated them."

He shakes his head. "I don't think you told me about her."

"Oh, I know I didn't."

"Why not?"

"Because I didn't tell anybody. I don't think she did either. It was so bloody awful. It was during a hunting party and it was in the woods and I was wet and itched for days after. I thought I'd sat on some sort of poisonous plant and my bits were going to shrivel and fall off."

"I don't think that's how it works."

I give him a sideways look. His mouth puckers. "It was bad, that's why I didn't tell you. It was bad and short and embarrassing. And my father had his dogs running around and I was petrified one of them was going to come across us and start baying."

"Oh God." Percy's eyes widen. "Those hounds were monsters."

"Thank you! Felicity loved them."

He shudders, then looks over at me again. "Why Amelia?"

I shrug. "She was there. And willing. And hated her freckles. And because my father was calling me a bitch every time I missed a shot or got knocked over by the recoil. God, I hate hunting. I hate guns. Men my size were not meant to be firing rifles. I'm far too small and delicate."

"Yes, those are most certainly two words I would use to describe you." He picks up a stone from the ground and tosses it over the edge of the cliff. We both wait for the splash, then he says, "Who was the first lad, then?"

"Ah." I scratch the back of my neck. "You don't want to know that."

"I do."

"You won't like it."

"I know I won't, but tell me anyway."

I could lie. But that's also something I'm trying to do less of. "Richard Peele."

He sucks in his cheeks, then lets out what I think is meant to be a sigh but comes out more like a growl. "No."

"I'm sorry."

"No!"

"I'm so sorry!"

"I hate Richard Peele."

"WE HATE RICHARD PEELE!" I shout to the sea. He snorts, and I press my forehead into his shoulder.

He touches his lips to the top of my head, then says, "Do you believe me when I tell you that I love you?"

"Sometimes." I keep my face pressed against him. "Mostly. I try to."

"Do you trust me?"

"Do *you* trust *me*?" I counter.

"Not always," he replies, and the honesty catches me off guard. I had expected to have to tease that out of him. "But I'm going to work on that, if you will."

"Trusting you?"

"Trusting yourself. And me, but we'll start with you." He cups his hands around my cheeks and raises my face to his. "You think I don't know all this about you? You think I couldn't see you falling apart when we were talking to Scipio about London and what we do now? And you don't think I was thinking, 'Damn it, now Monty's in his own head and we were supposed to have sex and that's probably ruined'? You don't think every time I said how much it meant to be together I didn't immediately regret it because you looked so panicked and I knew I was putting too much pressure on you and, dear God, Percy, just don't talk anymore, but I couldn't stop saying it? Because that was all I could think about last night."

"You fooled me."

His hands fall away from my face. "I think you were worrying about yourself."

"Sorry."

"I didn't mean it as a bad thing. But . . . I know you. And you know me. That's why we're here." He reaches out and touches his finger to the dimple on my right cheek until I smile. "And if you don't want to do this yet, that's fine. If you don't want to ever do it, that's fine too."

"Well, that sounds very unfun."

"But I mean it." He puts his hand on my knee. "And maybe we can't make it work. But maybe that doesn't matter because we're tough and we're stupid and we're going to try anyway."

I look down at his hand and laugh without quite knowing why. "You deserve a reward for all I put you through."

"You're my reward."

"What a rotten reward I am."

"Not to me. Why do you think everyone needs some sort of recompense for being around you?" he says, his voice so gentle I almost start to cry. He wraps an arm around me, pressing me against his chest, and I can feel the light touch of his hand on the back of my neck, fingers stroking my hair. "You don't owe me sex. You don't owe me anything. I'm with you because I want to be. And if we're *together*, it'll be because we both want to be. And we are going to London together because we want to. And it's going to be a disaster. But that's all right, because we'll have each other, and there's no one on this goddamn planet I'd rather be a disaster with than you."

I tip my head onto his shoulder, and he leans against

mine, and we look out over the ocean. Neither of us says anything for a while. I'm not sure how to believe any of that. How to break from the grooves I've worn down inside myself from years of thinking I'd never be anything more than a last resort.

But here is Percy. Here we are.

He stands suddenly, using his hand on my knee to push himself up. Then he steps out of his slippers and begins fumbling with the cuffs of his shirt. "Oh, are we going to try this again right now?" I ask, leaning backward against the rock.

"No, no. Keep your trousers on. For now." He holds out a hand to pull me up. "Come here."

I do not take it. "Tell me what you're doing first."

"You trust me, remember?"

"This is a trick question."

"Maybe. Is it a question?"

"It's definitely a trick."

"Come on, stand up." He peers over the edge of the cliff we're sitting on, which is when I realize what it is he's about to bully me into.

"Oh no. Absolutely not." I grab onto the edge of the rock I'm sitting on, like that will prevent me being dragged to the edge of the cliff and then inevitably over. "I'm not swimming, and I'm certainly not jumping into a swim. Do you know what's down there?" I point to the ledge he's standing on. "Water. *Water*, Percy. Also, possibly rocks."

"I dive here with Ebrahim and Georgie all the time. There are no rocks."

"Still, the best I can hope for is *water*, which there is nothing best about." He keeps that damn hand extended. I still don't take it. "You're actually going to force me to jump off a cliff to make a point about trusting you? That's a terrible abuse of this lovely chat we just had."

"I'm not going to make you do anything. But it's hot, and I want to swim, and I like seeing you flustered." He wiggles his fingers. "It's adorable."

And then he smiles. That full, bright smile that crinkles his nose just a bit. And what the hell am I supposed to do with that?

I take his hand.

He pulls me up, but I go no farther than that. We're so far apart that our fingers barely link. "Got to get a bit closer to the edge or you'll hit the rocks you're standing on when you jump," he says.

I take one step forward—still not close enough to get a clean leap into the ocean, but enough to peer farther over the edge. And then reel backward, my heart in my throat. "Son of a bitch, that's a long way down."

"It is not." He creeps closer to the edge of the cliff until his toes are nearly hanging over, then tugs at my hand. "Take your shoes off."

"If I leave them on, I can't jump, can I?" He pulls harder, defying gravity for a moment with my weight as a counter to his as he leans over the cliff, and I screech "Fine!" before he can drag me over. I kick off my slippers, then take two tentative steps up so our toes are aligned. I peer over the cliff once more and fight the urge to wrench backward. My heart is beating much faster than I think is healthy, and I'm starting to feel light-headed. "I can't do this."

"Yes, you can. Come on." He pulls me forward again, and I follow so slowly that I'm not entirely sure I'm actually moving.

"Are you going to let go of my hand?" he asks, and I realize I'm strangling his fingers.

"Absolutely not. Are you going to laugh at me if I hold my nose?"

"Only a little. Ready?"

"Could you give me a count—?"

And then Percy jumps, and I jump too, or rather, I am forced to jump too, and it turns out the only thing worse than hitting the water is the painful eternity before hitting the water as my brain screams all the way down, *THIS IS TOO FAR TO FALL AND LIVE.*

And then we hit the water, and no, this is far worse. I hate water. I hate swimming. It fills up my ears—ear—and my nose and burns the back of my throat. And I don't know which way is up and which is down; everything is white bubbles raised by our impact, and I can't open my eyes because the ocean is enormous and mean and it's hurting me.

And then I feel Percy's hand, which I am still clamped onto, tugging me upward. I can feel the light on my face.

My head breaks the surface, and I take a few gasping, grateful, burning lungfuls of air as I splash around, trying to swim before I realize that I am mostly afloat due to the fact that Percy is holding on to me. He's also laughing at me. "Stand up," he says.

"Too deep." A wave strikes me in the face, and I spit it all over Percy. He flinches with a laugh.

"It is not, there's a shelf here. Stand up."

I try to put my feet down, and my head goes under again. Percy pulls me back up to the surface, laughing harder. "My lord, you *are* too short!"

"You're too . . . mean!"

He's standing up, a little wobbly with the current, but he pulls me in to him, and lets me wrap my legs around him to keep my head above the water. The jump tugged his hair out of its knot, and it hangs heavy around his face. His wet skin shimmers where the sun strikes it. Beneath the waves, I can see the fine line of his collarbone bowing into his throat like the curve of a violin.

He licks his lips. There's a single drop of water perched upon the tip of his nose, and when it trickles down I am overcome with the same reckless desire that overtook me in Paris the first time we kissed. It quieted everything else inside me, all the constant clamor drowned out by the simple quiet of wanting him. Before the drop can fall back to the sea, I wrap my arms around his neck and catch it between our mouths.

It's like I've never kissed anyone before, and this is the first time I've ever been touched. His hands on my skin beneath the waves curl in, fingers digging into my spine. I rake my hands through his wet hair, pressing us together with such strength my back arches, and I am overwhelmed with how much I love him. It floods me and overflows. It feels like I made the ocean.

"Do you know what I would like to do?" I ask, my mouth still mostly against his so his tongue swoops against my teeth. "Right now."

"I hope it's unspeakable things to me."

I touch my nose to his. "That exactly."

"Right here?"

"God no. Get me out of this goddamn water."

I want to be the only thing touching him. I want to be the only thing that ever touches him again. I will be envious of every shirt he ever wears, the cuffs of his coats, the trousers going soft with wear where they rub his inner thighs. Every snowflake that ever falls upon his lips, every piece of bread upon his tongue. I want to breathe him, let him fill up my chest until my ribs strain and I break open like ripe fruit beneath a paring knife. I would be raw. I would freckle and blister in the sun. I would teach my body to regrow my heart each time I gave it to him, over and over and over again. Heart after heart after heart—every one of them his.

We drag ourselves from the ocean like kelp washed up on the shore, our bare feet leaving pulsing halos in the sand, and I can't stop looking at the way his wet trousers cling to the lines of his legs. I could write a god-damn opera in honor of his ass draped in thin cotton and the sea.

We both leave our slippers on the cliff—no time to go back for something so maudlin and unimportant—and stumble up the hill, hand in hand, then both my hands wrapped around his, then his arm around my neck and mine around his waist, tripping each other and laugh-ing at nothing and trying to touch each other as much as possible while still maintaining a somewhat coherent route back to the flat.

We leave sandy, soaking footprints up the cobbled path, riding an exuberant wind that's making us both giggly and wild. It feels like being drunk on the sweetest wine on earth.

"Is anyone here?" he whispers as we tumble into the still-silent courtyard, the sunlight just beginning to curl its fingers over the walls so everything looks soft and bright as a fresh oil painting.

"HALLO?" I call, then without giving anyone adequate

time to respond, turn to him. "No, no one's here."

"Quiet!" He claps a hand over my mouth, nearly tackling me but also grabbing me around the waist and lifting me off my feet. I let out a shriek of surprise, which shatters into a laugh, and I have just jumped off a goddamn cliff into the goddamn ocean, and we are tough and stupid together and we are going to be tough and stupid together for the rest of our lives.

I twist around in his grasp and press my mouth to his—colliding perhaps too much with teeth to be romantic, but he crooks an arm around my neck anyway and pulls me against him. He must have shaved this morning, because the skin along his jawbone is fawn-soft, the only stubble the sand still clinging to him. My hands find the small of his back, then lower, pressing our hips together. I can feel him lean into my grip, his head falling backward, and when I move against him, he grips my shoulder, like I'm holding him up.

"We should . . ." His words tumble into a sharp breath as I slot my knee between his legs. "Inside," he gasps. "We should go inside."

"Bedroom?" I ask.

"Bedroom," he confirms.

We stumble into the entryway, unwilling to release each other simply so we can walk upright. When I trip on the step up, Percy not only catches me, but somehow he manages to maneuver that catch into pressing me against the wall. It's like a goddamn magic trick how smoothly he does it. My soaked shirt makes a wet squelch against the plaster, and I start to laugh, and he starts to laugh with his lips against my throat, and I can't remember intimacy ever involving so much happy laughter before. He hoists me up, my legs around his waist so my head is higher than his, and I get the rare treat of leaning down to kiss him. I card my hands through his hair, pulling his mouth up to mine and sucking on his tongue as my shirt rucks up around my rib cage. His hand flexes against my bare skin, the other palming my thigh.

Somehow we get up to the bedroom. Smashing into everything. Cracking our elbows on every inch of the banister and leaving puddled footprints and collapsing against each other into the walls until finally we stumble into my bedroom, the door clacking against its frame behind us. It feels like a different room from the one we sat in stiffly the night previous, every furnishing mocking my uncertainties. The sunlight pouring through the open window makes the floor look polished, the bed-sheets silken and begging to be mussed. The whole room seems to be pleading with us to abso-bloody-lutely ravage it and not give a damn.

My hands go under his damp shirt and peel it up like shucking the skin off a fruit, our mouths together until we are forced to part so I can pull it over his head. I wrestle my own off, then let them both drop to the floor. When we come back together, it's his bare chest against mine, skin dewy, and my hands pawing at the waistband of his trousers. His breath grows heavy.

I'm too frantic for precision, and before I can get the buttons unfastened, Percy stumbles, the backs of his calves colliding with the bed, and he sits down with too much momentum, dragging me after him. The frame thuds into the wall so hard I actually think for a moment we might have snapped the ropes. Percy starts to laugh again, loud and heady. I could drink that sound forever and never again touch a bottle of spirits.

For a moment, we're too tangled to make sense of our own limbs, and then suddenly he's lying on his back and I'm on top of him. I pull myself up, straddling him with my knees pressed into his sides, our skin sticking everywhere we touch each other. I'm still wet, and already so sweaty from the heat and the exhilaration that there seems a good chance I may slide straight off. But every inch of me that isn't against him feels cold and incomplete.

I take his hands in mine. Our fingers twine, and I pin them above his head on the bed before pressing my lips against his chest. I love the way he moves against my mouth, the in and out of his breath, the clench of his muscles in response to my tongue. He tastes of salt. He brings one of our linked hands down to wrap around the back of my neck, pressing me against him as I suck at his skin. My mouth slips lower down his stomach, and I can feel myself starting to lose control, so I pause, surface for air, and ask, "Are you sure you want to do this?"

"Why?" He looks rosy and flushed, and I swear I can see the throb of his pulse in his throat. "Do you not?"

"No I'm just trying to . . ." I take a breath, which comes out more like a dramatic gasp. "Pace myself."

"You don't have to."

"Yes, really? I mean, really, yes, now?"

He licks his lips, then nods. I reach for the buttons on

his trousers, but he cries, "Wait!" And I freeze, panicked I've done something else to muck this up, but then he says, "Just . . . slowly, yes? Maybe not . . . a full game of backgammon just yet."

And then every inch of him goes red.

"Percy Newton." I sit up over top of him and cross my arms. When he looks back at me with his eyes wide and innocent, I parrot, *"A full game of backgammon?* What erotic leaflet did you pick up that filthy vocabulary from?"

"None!" he protests, but his mouth twitches. "Some."

"Some?"

Impossibly, he goes redder. "Some erotic leaflets."

"May I have their titles? For purely academic purposes, I assure you."

"Stop it." He pokes me in the stomach. "I wanted to prepare."

"Well you get top marks on that homework, darling," I say, letting myself tip forward onto his chest with my chin resting upon my stacked fists. "So if you're not ready to play backgammon quite yet, do you prefer playing something else? Bagpipes, perhaps?"

I expect a laugh, but instead his pupils dilate, turning his eyes almost black. I feel his breath catch beneath my fingers. Clearly we've been reading the same leaflets. "Yes, please."

"Lucky for you, I know a few songs." I kiss him on the tip of his nose, or rather I aim for that, but we're both a little shaky and I more sort of smash my teeth up his nose.

It is not technically necessary for both of us to be entirely naked for this particular duet, but there's a vulnerability that comes from being the only one completely undressed that I don't want to put him through. And, though I've lost some weight and still have lingering patches of skin peeling unflatteringly off my shoulders from where the sun had its way with me, I want him to see me.

I try to get my trousers off without actually climbing off him, but when I lift up one knee, I snag my foot in the cuff and pitch face-first into his chest, ending up collapsed flat against him with my trousers half on. Percy's weighted breathing breaks into a laugh. I feel his back arch under me with it, and before I can collect myself, he wraps his arms around me, pinning me to his chest. "You are such a goose, you know that?"

I laugh too, and bury my face in his neck. We lie

like that for a minute, breathing together, our skin gritty from sand and sticky with sweat. He's so warm against me, and the frantic pounding of wanting suddenly calms, then deepens, and with a breath I feel myself settle into him like lying in soft snow and leaving an imprint the shape of your body.

And then he says, "Are you going to take your trousers the rest of the way off?"

"Why?" I prop my chin up on his chest, suddenly feeling languid and teasing. We have time. We have our whole lives. "Are you excited?"

"I'm just assuming you wore your best underthings for me, and I'm quite keen to see them."

"Fooled you," I say as I slide off him, "because I'm not wearing any."

I do not attempt to undress overtop of him again—I peel myself away and step out of my trousers. He watches me, eyes tracing the lines of my chest, my shoulders, my stomach, and then dropping lower. He swipes the corner of his mouth with his thumb.

It all goes far more as I pictured it when I climb back over him, hook my fingers in the waistband of his trousers and slide them off him, his hips rising to follow me. And with every new inch of his skin that comes into view, all I can think is *Oh God oh God oh God this is actually going to happen oh my God how have I never noticed that his hipbones do that V thing oh my God it's Percy and we're here and oh my God if you invoke the name of the Lord further, you will deconsecrate this place.*

I wish I could travel backward in time and tell Monty of two years ago, lying on the lawn of his father's house with a black eye and a dawning realization he was falling in love with his best friend, that someday he'd be here. It would be years of drinking too much, falling asleep calculating how much arsenic he'd have to take to make certain the job was done, letting himself be groped by strangers in the backrooms of bars.

Maybe I'd go even further back than that—to Monty at twelve, or thirteen. That masturbating little bastard could have used a good buoying up, a promise to carry in his pocket that it wouldn't always be loneliness and hard hits and worrying he was catching some venereal disease from a girl he'd just met. Someday, you little twat, I'd tell him, it's going to be more. It's going to be better, and so will you. Where we start doesn't have to be where we end up.

Percy lets out a soft whine when I touch the inside of his thigh, first with just the tips of my fingers, then an exploratory palm. I nearly lose my mind at the sound. His back arches as I move upward, muscles tightening beneath me. My mouth goes suddenly dry, and my heart feels like it's beating so hard he can probably feel it in my kneecaps. His legs twist around my hips, one hand digging into my back as he pushes me down to him, the other strangling the bedsheets like they're a mooring line.

I remember suddenly the preparations I had made without Felicity's help for the night previous, and pause, fumbling for the drawer of the end table. "Hold on."

"Why?" he says, and it comes out a little petulant and a little nervous. It's a delicious combination.

"I've got a liniment."

As I lean over him, he slaps my stomach lightly. "You're *very* prepared."

"Well, yes, it was going to be a big night, if you remember—there were figs." I snatch the bottle from the drawer, then coat my hands until they're slick and fragrant. It takes me three tries before I get the bottle upright on the table, and when I crawl back over top of him, my hands soapy, I pause. He's looking at me—just looking—so hungry and anxious and bright and *mine*. What sort of stroke of miraculous luck brought me here? Brought me him?

I reach out before I can stop myself and push his hair behind his ears, then lean down for a kiss. When our lips meet, I swear I feel my ribs strain from how full I am with loving him.

But when I move downward again, Percy flinches, one hand flying to his face. "Hold on, wait, I've got something in my eye."

"What?"

"Something's in my eye."

"Like dust?"

"No, like . . . burning. I think it's whatever you've got on your hands."

"Damn it, sorry—"

"It's fine—"

"Here, let me see. Stop rubbing it so I can—"

He wicks his hand away from his eye just as I lean in, and his elbow collides with the side of the face, hard enough that I'm knocked sideways. I try to grab the bedpost, but my hands are so slippery that I slide right off and crash to the floor, my head connecting painfully with the corner of the drawer I left open. The bottle of oil falls off the edge and shatters into a soupy, amber pool.

"What happened? Are you all right?" Percy's got one eye open but blinking frantically, hand extended blindly to me.

"I'm fine." I touch the back of my head and it comes back damp and red. "No, wait, I'm bleeding."

"You're bleeding?" he yelps.

"It's fine!"

"It's clearly not if you're bleeding!"

I can feel a trickle down the back of my neck and I clap my hand against it, like I can force the blood to stay inside me if I just press tightly enough. "It's fine." My wrist is wet, and I look just as a drizzle of blood courses down my arm and into the crook of my elbow. "God, this is really bleeding." My vision swims, and when I reach to steady myself, I put my hand straight into the oily puddle of liniment, and I crash backward onto the floor.

Percy tries to come to my aid, but with one eye closed, he misjudges where he places his foot and steps on me. I screech and he slips, one leg tangled up in the sheets, and then suddenly the bedroom door bangs open and there's

Scipio, and I scream and Percy screams and Scipio lets out a horrified gurgle and then Felicity appears behind him in the doorway, claps her hands over her eyes, tries to run with her hands still covered, and slips in one of the dripping puddles we left on the stairs. Her feet go out from under her and she lands flat on her back at the top of the stairs, hands still valiantly clapped over her eyes.

Which rather ruins it all.

SEVEN

For the second time in a month, Felicity stitches my head closed.

It is remarkable how much calmer she was under the threat of my actual death than she is in the face of having accidentally walked in on my attempted deflowering of Percy. Or perhaps she's just being more enthusiastic about her stabbing than before as revenge for me being careless and forcing her to see what I'm fairly certain was more than a sliver of my naked backside.

When she's finished, she deposits me on the stoop of the house—my weak-and-wounded excuse once again trotted out as everyone else cleans up the somehow fantastic mess we made—with instructions to keep my head between my knees, a compress over my stitches, and to lie flat if I start to feel dizzy again. She's still red as an overripe beet when she leaves me.

After a while, Scipio comes and sits beside me, and then it's my turn to blush. I can't even look at him, and before he can say anything, I blurt out, "I'm so sorry."

"What for?" he asks.

"That you . . . saw that. And that we were . . ." I try to meet his eyes but lose my nerve at the last minute and duck back to staring at my feet. "In my defense, we were left unsupervised."

I don't know what I'm expecting from him, but it's not the casual shrug he offers. "When you spend months on the sea with only men, you're no stranger to sodomy. Believe me. Plenty of sailors take up with each other, and you're not the first I've interrupted by mistake. So you've not shocked me. And you've not surprised me either." I look up at him too quickly and my vision swims. He puts a steadying hand on my shoulder. "If you thought I was ignorant as to the nature of your relationship with Mr. Newton, you may need to reexamine your concept of appropriate physical fondness between friends."

I nod, trying to pretend it's fine when really my muscles are clenched and I'm fighting the urge to run. I don't want to have this conversation. I don't know where it's going, but my instincts tell me to scoot away from it. I can feel my shoulders rise, and perhaps he notices, for he lets his hand fall away and instead folds them in his lap. Perhaps it's only in my own mind, but it feels like a deliberate gesture, as though he's putting his hands away to show he won't raise them against me.

"We aren't *that* obvious," I say, and when Scipio gives me a pointed look, I add, "I know plenty of lads who are fond without being unchaste."

"But it's clear you're not those lads." I'm not sure if he hears the way my breath hitches, for he adds quickly, "Which is fine. Who gives a fig for chastity anyway?" He laughs at his own joke, glancing over at me like he's hoping I might join in. I wonder suddenly if this is what it's meant to be like, with a father and a son and a first real love. I can't imagine what this conversation would have been like with my actual father. Or rather, I can, because we had variations on it, but recalling them makes me want to put my hands up. Instead, I clench them against the knees of my trousers and take a breath before telling myself to relax. Let my hands fall loose and stop their trembling.

Trust him.

Scipio clears his throat into his fist, then continues, "I wouldn't have come in at all, but I could hear things crashing and something about blood and there were puddles all over the stairs."

"We were swimming. And wet. But not wet as in—it was water—I swear—and then I cut my head because—you know what, it doesn't matter."

Scipio runs a hand over his beard, then stretches his legs out straight in front of him. "You could have told me. I know it's been chaotic, but we could have given you two some time to yourselves."

I laugh—one short, humorless burst. "What would I have said—could you vacate the apartments for a while so Percy and I can engage in illegal activities?"

"Not illegal."

"They are where I come from." I shake my head, staring down at my feet. "I couldn't have. I've been struck too many times."

"Then maybe I should have said it to you sooner—you needn't hide around us," he says. "I'm sorry you ever felt you had to. And that the world makes you feel as though you have to." I finally manage to look up at him, and he smiles. I almost start to cry. Perhaps he senses it, for he claps a hand against my back brusquely, then stands. "I'm walking Miss Montague down to the ship for breakfast. She's quite fairly not interested in being here. I'd suggest you take it easy for a bit. The room is cleaned up, if you want to go back to bed."

"I'm going to sit here for a bit, I think."

"Suit yourself."

He starts to walk away, and I open my mouth to call out an apology, but instead what comes out is "Thank you."

He pauses. Turns back to me. Smiles again. "We have to look out for each other, Mr. Montague," he says. "It's the only way."

Scipio leaves me, and a few minutes later, I hear the front door open and shut. When someone sits down beside me again, I assume it's Felicity back to check on my progress before she leaves but then I feel a light touch on my back and Percy says, "Still bleeding?"

"No. Can you see out of both eyes?"

"Indeed I can. Look at us, healing rapidly."

I raise my head so I can rest my cheek on his shoulder, and he presses a kiss to the top of my head. He's fastened his hair back again, but I can smell the salt still tangled in it. We are still for a moment, the courtyard quiet but for the mumbling of the waves below us and the wind sighing through the trees. The island in conversation with itself.

"This was a disaster," I murmur.

I expect he'll deny it or say something cheerful to make me feel better, but instead he says, "Yes. It was a disaster."

I let out a short laugh of shock.

"But aside from all the disastrous elements," he goes on, "I was having a rather good time."

"Really?" I ask, failing to keep the surprise out of my voice. I raise my head, and he turns to me.

"Well." He tries to look serious, though I can see the smile hiding at the corners of his mouth. "There were figs."

"I love you," I say quietly. "You know that?"

"And I you, my darling boy." He nestles his head against mine and takes a deep breath. "Did Scipio go?"

"I think so."

"Felicity's gone too."

A telling pause.

I raise my head. "Percy Newton. Are you suggesting what I think you are?"

"I'm suggesting . . ." He looks over at me, the way his mouth curls somehow both a little shy and a little wicked—and that smile alone, it's enough. It's so much more than enough. "It's never going to be perfect."

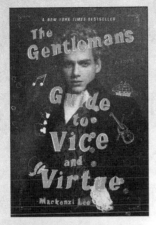

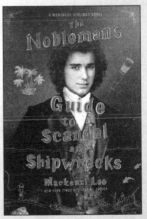

JOIN THE
Epic Reads
COMMUNITY